This igloo book belongs to:

……………………………………

igloobooks

Written by Stephanie Moss
Illustrated by Emanuela Mannello

Designed by Alex Alexandrou
Edited by Caroline Richards

Copyright © 2018 Igloo Books Ltd

First published in the UK by Igloo Books Ltd
An imprint of Igloo Books Ltd
Cottage Farm, NN6 0BJ, UK
Owned by Bonnier Books
Sveavägen 56, Stockholm, Sweden

All rights reserved, including the right of reproduction
in whole or in part in any form.

Manufactured in China. 0121 002
10 9 8 7 6 5 4 3 2 1

Library of Congress Cataloging-in-Publication
Data is available upon request.

ISBN 978-1-83903-745-0
IglooBooks.com
bonnierbooks.co.uk

Eva just loved unicorns. She thought about them all day long. If anyone said they weren't real, she was sure that they were wrong.

Unicorn toys in her bedroom were in piles ten feet high.

And she longed to see one flying gracefully up in the sky.

Eva had a pretty pony that she played with every day. She'd pretend she was a unicorn. "Fly, Sparkle, fly," she'd say.

"But unicorns don't exist," all Eva's friends giggled with glee.

"Come to my special party," she said. "Just you wait and see!"

The stables were all decorated in pink, purple, and green. It was the most enchanting party that Eva had ever seen!

Before her friends arrived, Eva kissed Sparkle's soft, warm head.

"I wish you REALLY were a unicorn," she closed her eyes and said.

Then all of a sudden, her pony began to glow. Wings and a horn appeared, and rainbow hair started to grow!

The stunning unicorn was far beyond her wildest dreams. She twinkled like the stars and looked as pretty as moonbeams.

Sparkle's voice was soft and gentle.
She said, "Let's fly off on the breeze!"
Eva climbed up on her back, as she cried,
"WOO-HOO! WHEE! Yes, please!"

"Your magic kiss transformed me," explained Sparkle, as they flew. "Most people don't believe in us. Most people aren't like you."

They glided past a rainbow on marshmallow clouds of white.
Then far off in the distance, something gleamed in the sunlight.

Eva saw a magic palace and,
as she looked all around,
Sparkle shook her mane and smiled,
landing gently on the ground.

The other unicorns were playing at the forest waterfall. Eva thought they were so beautiful she had to meet them all!

"I'm Shimmer," said one unicorn. "I'm Moonshine," said one more.

Their beauty was like nothing she had ever seen before.

To celebrate her visit, they brought her treats of every kind.
There were so many things to choose from, but Eva didn't mind!

"I hope my party is this good," she said.
"We'd all have so much fun."
With just one swish of Sparkle's tail,
Eva's special wish was done.

When it was time to go, Sparkle flew Eva through the stars.
"What a magical adventure," said Eva, "and it's all ours."

Back home, she kissed Sparkle and said, "Thank you," in her ear.

Sparkle turned back into a pony, then Eva saw her friends appear.

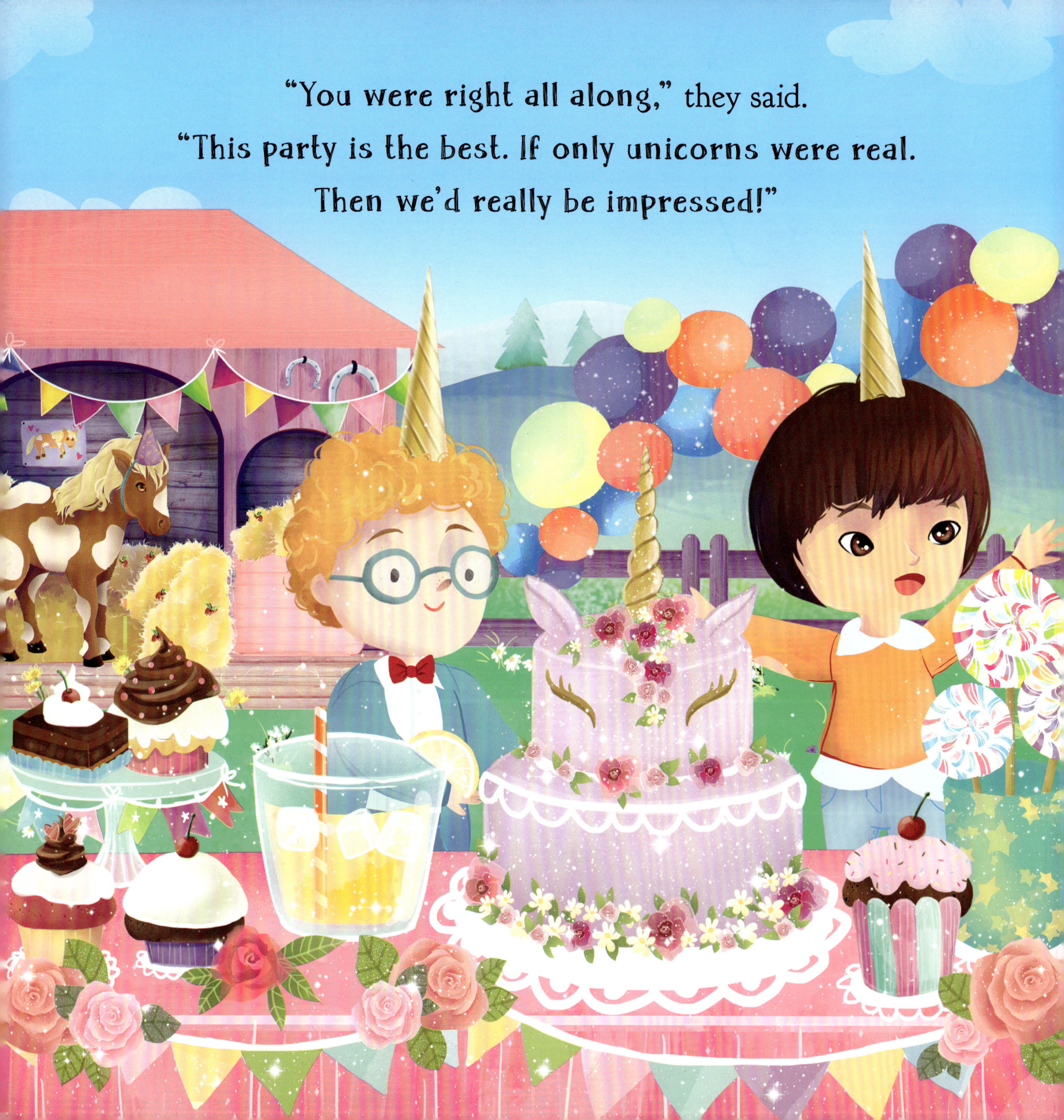

"You were right all along," they said.
"This party is the best. If only unicorns were real.
Then we'd really be impressed!"

Eva gave a secret smile and she winked at Sparkle, too.
"You just have to believe," she said.
"Then your wish will come true."